CW01271910

BOTH
PUBLISHING

Published in 2021 by BOTH Publishing.

The author asserts their moral right to be identified as the author of their work, in accordance with the Copyright, Designs and Patents Act, 1988.

Copyright © Stan Nicholls 2021.
All rights reserved.

This book is sold subject to the condition that no part may be reproduced, distributed, or transmitted in any form or by any means, including photocopying, recording, or other electronic or mechanical methods, without the prior written permission of the publisher.

A CIP catalogue record of this book is available from the British Library.

ISBN - 978-1-913603-00-7
eBook available - ISBN - 978-1-913603-01-4

Printed in the UK by TJ Books Limited.
Distributed by BOTH Publishing.

Cover design by Chrissey Harrison and Alistair Sims. Typeset by Chrissey Harrison.

Part of the Dyslexic Friendly Quick Reads Series.

www.booksonthehill.co.uk

ANCHOR POINT

Stan Nicholls

Other dyslexic friendly quick read titles from BOTH publishing

The House on the Old Cliffs

Ultrasound Shadow

The Clockwork Eyeball

At Midnight I Will Steal Your Soul

The Breath

Sherlock Holmes and the Four Kings of Sweden

The Man Who Would Be King

Anchor Point

"*Draw* it, boy! Put some *effort* into it! And straighten that arm!"

Kye could feel his hands shaking as he fought to keep the bow at full stretch and level.

"Watch your stance!" Harper added, emphasising the point by firmly pushing Kye's hip into the correct position.

A trickle of sweat made its way down Kye's brow. He struggled to curb the trembling as he eyed the target.

"Anytime today," Harper remarked sarcastically.

Kye loosed the arrow. It struck the boss, just a hundred paces distant, but nowhere near the bull.

Glimm Harper gave him a look combining exasperation and pity. He turned to the other dozen or so band members and signalled for them to stop practising. "All right, that's enough for now!" To Kye, he said, "You need to concentrate more. A hell of a lot more. I'll be talking to you about this later."

He headed off in the direction of the village, leading the others.

As Kye started to collect his gear, someone gave him a hard shove from behind, toppling him. Huew Rignorr loomed over him, his face twisted with malice. He was getting on for four years older than Kye, and considerably more muscular. His dark hair was shaven to the point of being almost stubble, contrasting with Kye's flowing blond locks.

"Why don't you give it up, Beven?" he growled, piggy eyes blazing with spite. "Face it, you're a disgrace to the band."

Kye's timorous mumbled protest was cut off with a contemptuous slash of Rignorr's hand. "Shut it, you little sniveler."

For a moment, Kye thought Rignorr was going to hit him again, but with a last baleful glare, he left.

Dusting himself off, Kye carried on collecting his kit, eyes stinging.

Dyan Varike approached. She was one of the best archers in the band and the only member who seemed to have time for Kye, perhaps because there was no more than a season's difference in their ages.

"Don't take any notice of him," she said, directing a sour look at the departing Rignorr.

Kye wiped the back of a hand across his eyes and managed a weak smile. "I try not to."

"Yeah, well, try harder."

"That's easily said."

"I know it's difficult, with Huew being the elder's son and all, but—"

"Can we not talk about him? Please?"

She shrugged. "All right." Her lengthy red hair had been tied back during practice. Now she undid it, and with a shake of her head her hair tumbled free. "Come on, let's get home."

They walked to the targets to retrieve Kye's arrows, then towards the village, trailing the rest of the band.

Winter's last traces were gone, and Spring had taken a hold. Early flowers of yellow and white dotted the verges of the path they trod. Following an overnight shower, the scent of new growth and revitalized soil perfumed the air.

To their left and rear stretched the forest, vast and dense, and the mountains beyond could just be seen, peaks still dusted with snow. Ahead, the ground sloped downwards and would take them to the shallow valley where Catterby lay, a village that had grown over the years and now more closely resembled a small town. The forest, the valley, and remoteness conspired to conceal the place, and an outsider might not even realise a settlement was there.

"You can do it, you know," Dyan said.

"What?"

"Master the bow."

"Oh, that."

"Yes, *that*."

"You seem to be the only one who thinks so."

"Not true, Kye. Glimm can see your potential."

"He's got a funny way of showing it."

"He wouldn't have you in his band if he thought you were useless."

"Huew thinks I am. Probably the

others do, too."

"Forget them. If Glimm seems hard on you, it's only because he can see what's holding you back."

"And what's that?"

"That it's not talent you lack, but confidence."

He thought about that and replied, "Maybe the real problem's that I don't want to be in the band."

"You know that service in one branch or another of the defence force is compulsory, and this band's pretty much the elite. You should be proud you were picked for it."

"Should I?"

"*Yes!* It's a dangerous world out there. A lot of Gerrik's in turmoil from what we've heard. We have to protect ourselves from that."

"But nobody thought to ask me what part I wanted to play."

"It doesn't work like that. You're stuck with the way things are. You've no choice but to make the best of it."

"Maybe I do have a choice."

"Not as long as you live in Catterby you don't, and ... hang on. You're not thinking of running away, are you? Because that'd be really—"

A commotion ahead cut her short. The other band members had stopped and were agitated about something. Kye and Dyan sprinted to them.

"What's up?" Dyan wanted to know.

"Strangers, in the village," Glimm

Harper told her. "And they don't look too friendly."

※

Harper quietened them all. Moving stealthily, the band crept forward to join the couple of lookouts already on a wooded ridge overlooking the village. Lying low, they could see the main square.

Five black-clad horsemen were there, facing a gathering crowd. The one leading them was thin to the point of cadaverous and sported a shock of black hair and a neatly trimmed goatee, unlike his companions, who were hairless, brawny, and bore an unhealthy pallor. None of the riders dismounted, and their expressions were stern.

"Who is the Elder here?" the leader demanded.

A stocky, balding man stepped forward. "I am."

"And you are?"

"Toray Rignorr." His tone, like his appearance, was portentous. "The question is, who are *you*?"

"Eskail Gudreen, Emissary."

"Emissary for who?"

"My lord Salex Nacandro. I take it you've heard of him?"

A shocked murmur went through the crowd. The Elder was taken aback at the mention of the name and seemed lost for words. Another man emerged from the throng and moved to face the strangers.

Up on the ridge, Dyan said, "That's your father, isn't it?"

Kye nodded, anxious.

Huew Rignorr grasped Harper's arm and hissed, "We should be down there."

Harper pried loose his grip. "Hold your horses," he whispered. "If we charge in we could make things worse."

"But—"

"*Quiet*. It's hard enough to hear as it is."

Huew didn't like it, but held his peace and fumed silently.

Down below, the Emissary surveyed Kye's father as though he were a bug fit only for the heel of his boot. "Ah, I see we have another spokesman. One who hasn't lost his tongue, I trust, unlike your Elder. Do you have authority here?"

"I'm Seth Beven, and I have the authority of a concerned citizen."

Gudreen gave a mirthless laugh. "How very egalitarian."

"What business does your lord have with Catterby?"

"Allow me to correct you. The proper expression is *our* lord."

"There you're mistaken. We serve no lords in this quarter of Gerrik."

"Then it's time you did."

Another, louder murmur rose from the crowd, which was growing.

Elder Rignorr recovered some of his

poise. "What are you saying?"

"Lord Nacandro has greatly expanded his ... sphere of influence in recent times."

"Yes, we've heard," Seth Beven responded cynically.

The Emissary ignored him. "And he wishes to extend the prosperity and security afforded by his rule."

"We have all the prosperity and security we need."

"I beg to differ. Be advised that this district, including your village, is now under a new master."

That brought more tumult from the villagers Elder Rignorr, Seth Beven, and a score of others added their yelled protests to the din.

"Enough!" the Emissary roared. "I can see that this dismal backwater is sorely in need of a taste of discipline!" His tunic parted as he rose angrily in the saddle, affording a glimpse of a pendant at his chest, secured with a silver chain. It was black, and at its centre lay a crimson gem, shining with an unnatural intensity.

The Emissary lifted a hand but did no more than point. A blistering, golden ray flashed to a nearby lodge and instantly set it ablaze. A hay wagon, his next target, flipped over as it ignited. A stockade fence burst into flames, the cattle within taking noisy fright.

The villagers took fright too. Amid screams and shouts they scattered. Some fell, some transformed into shrieking fireballs, their clumsy flight adding to the flames as they blindly collided with windbreaks and shrubbery. A billowing, acrid smoke began to amass.

Emissary Gudreen regarded the scene with something akin to indifference, punctuated with an occasional smirk of amusement.

Kye lost track of his father in the melee below and found that he was tightly clutching Dyan's arm, though she seemed unaware of it, or accepting.

The rest of the band were unnerved, and Harper was trying to calm them. "This is what training's for!" he reminded them, his voice betraying a hint of his own alarm. For all their drilling, the band had never engaged in actual combat, and more than half of them were barely on the threshold of man and womanhood.

Harper himself was no longer young. "Let's see what they make of a volley – but we'll do it in good order!"

To fire, they had to stand, and no one needed the risk pointing out. Harper quickly got them organised as best he could, forming a line along the lip of the ridge.

"On my word you rise, draw, shoot, and drop!" he ordered. "Don't linger, just do it! Understood? And don't hit our own!"

They nocked their arrows, many with unsteady hands.

Kye's heart was racing. Dyan crouched next to him. He gave her a look and she returned it, their gaze locked for an eternal instant. There was nothing to say.

Keeping low, Harper scurried along the line, checking kit, patting backs, and squeezing arms. Reaching the end, he cautiously straightened and looked below. The view was brief. Dropping to his knees, he charged his own bow. "Remember what I said!" he called. "Be swift!"

Kye was worried that he wouldn't have the courage to stand when the order came. He worried whether, if he did, his shot would be of any use. And he worried about the distinct possibility of dying. He glanced at Dyan. She looked grim, maybe a little fearful, but with something else in her expression that spoke of determination. He knew there was no question of her not doing what had to be done. It gave him heart.

Muscles tensed, they waited.

"Steady, steady," Harper cautioned. "When I say ... *Now!*"

They leapt up, one or two half stumbling, drawing their strings as they rose. Huew Rignorr let out a roar as he straightened, a few others feebly echoing him.

Kye and Dyan were on their feet at just about the same time, their bows already taut. What they saw was chaos. Buildings burned, their flames illuminating scattered bodies. The golden beam flashed and another dwelling loudly detonated.

Some people still staggered or ran about the square, mingling with liberated cattle amid the choking smoke. Through its tendrils, Kye made out the Emissary and his minions, issuing destruction from horseback.

He took a breath, held it, aimed, and loosed the bolt. Dyan's arrow matched his for speed. No more than three heartbeats had passed, but even as they dropped back to hiding, they knew it was useless.

They had seen the band's stream of arrows winging down, and saw them transformed into streaks of flame and ash as they struck some unseen barrier protecting their targets.

"Gods, what now?" someone exclaimed. "How can we fight magic with bows?"

Others joined the chorus. Harper was trying to still them when a garbled shout came from along the line. They turned to its source. Ansger, one of the older and nervier band members, had braved a look at the scene below. He shouted again. "*Watch out!* Those ... henchmen are coming!"

Harper, Kye, and Dyan dared a peek, along with a handful of others. Four figures were silhouetted against a backdrop of flames. They were on foot and already halfway to the base of the ridge.

"Another volley," Harper decided.

"The last did no good," Huew griped.

"Do you have a better idea? No, I thought not."

"It's worth a try," Kye said.

Huew scowled at him. "Who cares what you think, you scum-sucking—"

"*Shut it,*" Harper told him. "The distance is shorter than our last shot. And it's his bodyguard, or whatever they are, not the Emissary himself. He's the one using magic."

"Could make a difference," Dyan ventured.

"We'll have to hope it does. Now get back in line." He eyed Huew. "All of you."

They moved to take up their positions.

"On my word," Harper said. "Take as careful aim as you can. But don't be an age doing it. Right?" He paused ever so briefly, casting his gaze along the line. "*Now!*"

Kye thought that the second time might be easier. It wasn't. There was still the dark certainty that lifting his head would make him lose it, and the dread that the last thing he'd see would be his village, his home, under attack. But he rose and drew, in step with Dyan beside him.

The group of black-clad figures was at the foot of the ridge now and starting up it. This close, it was possible to see the wickedly curved blades they carried. Kye was almost at the end of the line, so naturally, he targeted the one in direct sight, on the left side of the climbing group. He aimed square for the chest and loosed.

The arrow flew with the rest of the band's flock, swooping to pepper the climbers, when history repeated itself. Before they could reach their marks, the arrows encountered something that could not be seen but which dissolved them in fire. The four carried on climbing, unfazed.

"We need to retreat," Harper decided.

Kye said, "Surely there's something we can—"

"Against magic? No, we'd only be throwing our lives away. We fall back and regroup." He addressed the whole band: "Move as quickly and as quietly as you can. If any get separated, we'll meet in the clearing at Gall's Point, near the lake. Don't head straight there; take an indirect route. *Now go!*"

They ran. Pelting through the forest, panic barely suppressed, they were convinced that the Emissary's henchmen were at their heels. Every sound, every errant shadow, increased their fright and their pace. Along the way the band fragmented, some falling behind, others racing ahead. Fortunately, they all heeded Harper's words and took varying paths to Gall's Point.

When Kye and Dyan got to the rendezvous, it was growing dark. Most of the others were already there, with stragglers arriving in dribs and drabs. Harper was there, and a sour-faced Huew.

"I think we lost them," Dyan panted.

"Looks like it," Harper replied, scanning the treeline.

"What now?" Kye asked.

"Get some rest."

"That's it? Get some rest? What about our village?"

"We all have kin and friends down there, Kye, and we're all worried. But there's nothing we can do about it right now. So save your strength, you're going to need it."

Kye and Dyan nodded and left him, weathering a filthy look from Huew as they moved away. They found a corner of the clearing at the base of a broad, mature tree, and settled down.

"I don't know that we're doing the right thing," Kye said, "sitting here when the village needs us."

"It's hard. But I think Glimm's right. We did what we could, and you saw how futile that was. If we're going against these outsiders, we need to understand what we're facing."

"I suppose. But my parents are down there, and I'm not doing anything to help them."

"It's at times like this I'm glad I'm an orphan."

"Dyan, I'm sorry. I—"

"No, no, no. I'm not asking for sympathy. I'm just grateful that I don't have your problem. My grandparents raised me and they're long gone, as you know."

"Looks like the rest of the villagers are going to join 'em if that Emissary gets his way."

"I've been thinking about him. Maybe there's a limit to the magic he uses."

"How so?"

"Notice how he didn't fire any of

those golden beams at us when we were on the ridge? What did he do? He sent his henchmen after us instead of using magic."

"Hmmm, maybe. But he doesn't seem to have a limit when it comes to destroying Catterby."

"I don't think he'll destroy the entire village. Why would he? A desolate place is no use to his master, and it's a pretty good bet that getting on Salex Nacandro's wrong side isn't a great idea."

"He's bad, isn't he, this Nacandro?"

"You must have heard the rumours. He's feared as both a sorcerer and a warlord – not a good blend. Many have died because of him. Everybody seemed to think that, because his homeland's so far to the north, he'd never be a threat to these parts. Looks like that was wrong. But with someone like Nacandro—"

"With someone like Nacrando," Huew Rignorr said, coming into sight from the other side of the tree, "victory's assured if your enemies are weak." He gave Kye a pointed look. "From what I've heard, he admires strength."

"Is that what you think you are, Huew; strong?" Dyan asked.

He regarded her darkly. "Somebody has to be."

"I don't think we're weak," Kye volunteered. "It's just that—"

"Who gives a shit for *your* opinion, Beven? It's spineless types like you, and your precious father, who should have no part in the affairs of our village."

Kye rose. "That's not fair. My father—"

Huew punched him, hard. Kye reeled, blood seeping from his lip. He looked about to hit back but stayed his hand. Huew stormed off.

"What a bastard," Dyan said, handing Kye a cloth.

Kye dabbed at his lip. "I think that's a fairly accurate description."

"You all right?"

"I"ll live."

"Why is he so hard on you? Apart from being born a dickhead, that is."

"Well, he said it, didn't he? My father."

"From the time he ran against Huew's father for the Eldership? But Toray Rignorr won that contest. What's there to be sore about?"

"Toray won, but only just. My father got a lot of support, though not quite enough. I think Huew resents the idea of anybody standing against his clan."

"Well, I reckon your father would've made a much better Elder, if that counts for anything."

Kye managed a wincing smile. "It does."

"Let's do as Glimm said and get some rest, shall we?"

They bedded down as best they could, but sleep didn't come easily for either of them.

Their fitful night ended as dawn was breaking. Scouts returned and reported that Nacandro's Emissary and his party had left the village. Gathering their weapons, and heeding Harper's warning to be cautious, the band started for home.

They found a bleak scene when they arrived. Buildings were burnt out, fences were down, escaped cattle were being rounded up. The task of collecting bodies was underway, and the first funeral pyres were already alight. But Dyan had been right in assuming that the whole village hadn't been destroyed. The damage was bad but came nowhere near affecting the entire settlement, just enough to act as a warning.

The reactions the returning band got were mixed. Some of the townspeople thought them cowardly and were vocal about it. Other, wiser heads understood the reason for their absence. Most were too preoccupied with mourning their dead and clearing the devastation to care much either way.

No sooner had they arrived than Huew received news that his father, the Elder, had died in the attack. No one could gauge his feelings beneath the usual pall of anger he wore, and when Harper extended a comforting hand, Huew slapped it away. Wordless, his expression unreadable, he made for his family's lodge.

Kye was desperate for word of his own family. Those he asked either didn't know or were reticent in meeting his gaze. Fearing the worst, he dashed for home.

Dyan followed at a distance.

His mother, Magda, was in the Bevens' lodge, sitting alone in shuttered gloom. Her face lit when she saw him, and new tears were added to traces of the old.

"Kye, oh Kye," she sobbed as she embraced him. "I feared you'd been lost too."

"Too?" he said, his voice barely audible.

"Seth. Your father ... he ..." She couldn't go on but nodded at the door to the room where the family usually ate.

Kye didn't want to go in but knew he must. The door was slightly ajar. Steeling himself, he pushed at it and entered.

His father's body was laid out on the sturdy table. He'd been cleaned up, and the clothes he wore were his spotless best. There was no hiding the scars, bruises, and burns he bore on his face and hands. Kye tried not to think about how the rest of him looked.

Kye's own tears came then, and his mother joined him, sharing the anguish. After a long while, they left the room and Kye's mother explained how Seth had met his end. Kye wasn't surprised to hear that it involved his father trying to protect someone else, which was characteristic.

"I feel so bad that the band weren't here to help," he confessed.

"You can put that out of your mind right now," his mother told him. "I'm sure there was a good reason for it. As a matter of fact, I'm *glad* you weren't here. If you had been, you might have ended up like ... like ..." She broke down, and he held her.

When she calmed, she said, "They're coming back, you know, that devil of an Emissary and his thugs. They've given the village an ultimatum: surrender or else."

"When did they say they'd be back?"

"The next full of the moon."

"That's five days."

"Yes, no time at all. There's a meeting due around now to decide what to do about it."

"We need a meeting? Surely it's obvious. We have to resist."

"I can't bear the thought of losing another loved one, Kye. And there are plenty who feel the same."

"Surrendering to Salex Nacandro's force could be worse. This meeting. I don't want to leave you when things are like this, but—"

"No, you go. Go *on*, I'll be fine."

"Really?"

"It's what your father would have done. And the more I see of him in you, the more precious you are to me."

They embraced, and he left.

He found Dyan outside, perched on a rain barrel. She stood and put her arms around him. "I'm so sorry, Kye."

Again there were tears. When Kye gathered himself, he said, "You've heard that they're coming back?"

She nodded gravely. "They're having a meeting about it in the square, or what's left of it."

"I think we should fight. Agree?"

"*Of course.*"

"Some want to surrender. Maybe most of them."

"Then let's get to that meeting."

They dashed for the square.

It looked as though just about everyone was heading the same way, save for the badly injured and those caring for them. A number of people offered Kye their condolences as he passed, and the respect shown to his father went some way to thawing the chill in Kye's heart. Arriving at the square, Dyan and Kye weaved through the crowd to its centre, where a chaotic meeting was underway.

They ran into Glimm Harper. "I was

truly sorry to hear about your father," he said. "He was a good man."

Kye thanked him, and added, "How's this going?" He nodded at the arguing crowd.

"It's on a knife-edge. Those who want to surrender are making a passionate case, those against argue with just as much zeal. It could go either way."

Kye had hoped for a chance to speak, though the prospect would normally have scared him. But that was before he lost his father, and the probability that more would die and his village would become enslaved. In the event, he didn't get to speak. Too many others had something to say, or yell, and the clamour defeated any disciplined debate.

Eventually, most of the arguments were spent. With some effort, a vote was agreed and the crowd quietened. As it was about to be taken, Huew Rignorr barged through the mob and turned to face it.

"Most of you know that my father, our Elder, was lost yesterday," he announced in a voice loud enough to be heard by all. There were sounds of sympathy from some of his audience. "This could not have come at a worse time for our community. Now, more than ever, we need someone to lead us." Shouts of agreement and applause rippled the crowd. It was hard to tell if they outnumbered those who, suspecting what was coming next, stayed silent.

"He wouldn't, would he?" Dyan said.

"Oh yes he would," Kye reckoned.

"Given the crisis we're facing," Huew went on, "and the need for leadership, I believe that I should assume the position of Elder."

That brought cheers and boos, applause, and catcalls. Most members of the village council were present, consisting of Catterby's more prominent citizens. Few of them looked impressed by Huew's proposal. One stepped forward.

"Of course, we're sorry for your loss, Huew," he said, "but you know it's not an hereditary position."

"An election now would be a distraction," Huew replied, "a waste of time."

"Elections are never a waste of time.

Though, with the threat we face, I think all of us agree that now would not be the right time."

"Who will lead us then?"

"We have the council." He indicated the other notables.

"A headless chicken."

More ragged cheers and jeering from the crowd.

Another councillor stepped up. "And there's the question of your youth."

"That's what this place needs!"

"It also needs experience."

"Perhaps I can suggest a middle way," a third council member offered. "I propose that we hold not one but two votes: one on how we deal with

Nacandro's Emissary when he returns.; the other on whether Huew Rignorr should assume the role of Elder, on the clear understanding that the appointment would last only until an election can be held, and that said election should take place as soon as possible. Assuming, of course, that we're in a position to hold an election five days hence."

Not everyone was happy with that.

In the crowd, Harper whispered, "That's running a hell of a risk."

Dyan nodded. "Yeah, having Huew in charge for even a short time doesn't sound too bright an idea."

"And I wonder how easy it'd be taking away the Eldership once he'd got it," Kye said.

After some further noisy discussion, the two-vote option was agreed, and the councillor who first spoke conducted it.

"All those in favour of Huew Rignorr being appointed as *temporary* Elder, raise your hands. Now all those opposed."

Huew had his supporters, but those against the appointment numbered at least two-thirds of the crowd.

"I declare the opposers to be in the majority."

The losers raised a racket, drowned by the cheers of those against the proposal.

Red-faced with fury, Huew shouted, "*Fools!* You'll regret this!"

He plunged into the crowd, elbowing his way through to jeers and some exclamations of sympathy. It took a moment for everything to quieten down.

"To the second vote," the councillor announced. "All those in favour of accepting the ultimatum and yielding to Salex Nacandro's rule, indicate now." A number of hands went up. "And those who favour refusing and mounting a defence." Another forest of hands.

Unlike the previous vote, this was closer and needed a count of hands. The result was tight, but clearly in favour of refusal. Immediately the council began discussing plans and delegating tasks.

"That's a relief," Dyan said.

"Now we have to make sure our defences are up to the job," Kye replied.

"And that could be in the gift of the gods," Harper told them.

The next day saw Seth Beven's funeral. Many people turned out, attesting to his popularity, and even those who favoured the Rignorrs were represented. Huew Rignorr himself was absent, though few lamented the fact.

Magda Beven managed to say a few words about her late partner. Kye spoke too, praising his father's kindness, resolve, and dedication to his community. He also tried to convey what his father had meant to him, and the qualities he hoped he might have inherited. It was all Kye could do to get through that part.

Cuin Whanston, who acted as chief celebrant when it came to the village's spiritual affairs, commended Seth's spirit to the gods. Then Kye's mother applied a flame to the funeral pyre with shaking hands.

The Bevens weren't alone in being tearful, but the goodwill of their neighbours went some way to assuaging their grief, and Kye was especially grateful for Dyan's support.

Kye's way of keeping the sorrow at bay in the following couple of days was to throw himself into helping develop the village's defences. Huew Rignorr was nowhere to be seen during all the activity. He was assumed to be moping in his lodge, which only confirmed the opinion of those who had rejected him as Elder.

With time running out, the days were long and hard. At Kye's mother's insistence, Dyan and Kye took a rare break from their toil and enjoyed a proper meal at the Beven lodge.

Magda had also blanketed her sorrow by devoted herself to the defences, in her case by helping to prepare batches of measured rations against the possibility of a siege. As they ate, the trio discussed progress.

"At this rate, we should have enough supplies to hold out for quite some time," Magda said. "And thank the gods that we have wells within the village precincts. How are the physical defences going, Kye?"

"All right, I suppose."

"You suppose?"

"We're building barriers and laying traps. The blacksmiths are forging blades, and the band are working day and night turning out arrows."

"But?"

"Will it be enough against the power that Emissary has? We didn't come out of it too well last time, did we?"

"We can only do our best and hope we prevail."

"I think we've got to do better than that, Mother."

"What we need," Dyan reckoned, "is magic to combat magic. Then we might have a fighting chance Pity we have no sorcerers in Catterby."

"That's not entirely true," Magda said. "In a way."

"What do you mean?" Kye wanted to know.

"Well, there's Niola."

"Of course! I'd forgotten about her."

"Just a minute," Dyan said. "She's just an old woman living in solitude. We know she's thought of as wise, and she does have some curative skills, but a sorcerer?"

Kye shrugged. "Who knows what she's capable of? And what other option is there?"

"It's a long shot," Dyan said.

"It seems to me that it's our only shot." Kye pushed away his plate and got up. "If you'll excuse me, Mother."

"Where are you going?"

"To the council."

"You think they'd favour consulting Niola?"

"We won't know until we try. Coming, Dyan?"

"Try and stop me."

They made for the longhouse where the council was sitting in more or less permanent session, directing the defences. The place was abuzz, with plenty of people coming and going. After some delay, Kye and Dyan worked their way to the lengthy table where four or five councillors were seated.

"Ah, Kye," one said. "What can we do for you?"

"I don't want to waste your time, so I'll not waste words."

"Very well. Go on."

"We're all doing our best to build defences, but I'm doubtful they'll be enough to hold off the outsiders. We need magic to even the odds."

"And we have none to call upon. What's your point, Kye?"

"I think we just might."

That got their attention. "In what way?" one of the other council members asked.

"Niola."

A couple of the councillors laughed. The others just looked disappointed. "Are you serious?" someone asked.

"Yes. I know it's a venture but—"

"You can say that again. Whatever makes you think an old recluse could be of any help?"

Kye pointed at one of the men.

"Remember when she sent herbs that treated your daughter when she was poorly?" He pointed to another. "How she put right your cows when they wouldn't give milk? And—"

"That's all very well," a councillor said, "and we appreciated her aid. But herbalism and minor enchantments are no match for the kind of magic we're facing."

"Nevertheless, I'd like to consult her."

The council didn't even need to discuss the idea before giving their answer. One member spoke for them all. "It's heartening that you should be thinking so ... creatively about our plight. But we can see no merit in seeking help from Niola. Carry on with your work on the defences, Kye. That's how best to employ yourself."

There was no budging them. Kye and Dyan left.

Outside, Dyan sighed. "That's that then."

"Is it?"

"You heard what they said, Kye."

"I heard their *opinion*, yes. Whether I abide by it ..."

"You're going to seek out Niola, despite what they said?"

"I don't see any other option."

"Good. I'm coming with you."

"You don't have to do that, Dyan."

"I'm coming."

He smiled, quietly pleased that she'd be with him.

"One question," she said. "This isn't

really about running away, is it?"

Coming from her, he took no offence at the remark. "No. After what's happened lately, that's not on my mind any longer."

"Glad to hear it. What's the plan?"

"It's still quite early. We should be able to make the foothills before nightfall."

"So a day there, a day back."

"Just enough time to get home before the Emissary returns, barring mishaps."

"And likely nothing to show for it."

"Could be."

"All right. Let's see if we can get together enough food and water for the trip."

"We need to do that on the quiet, and not let anybody know what we're up to.

Understood?"

She understood.

They made good progress, at least at first. By midday the verdant terrain surrounding the village gave way to a meaner landscape and their pace dropped. They stopped just once, for a brief, frugal meal, and didn't make a fire.

The mountain they headed for loomed ever higher, and the ground underfoot grew stonier. At last, as night was beginning to fall, they reached the foothills. As neither Kye nor Dyan had ever been there before, there was some frustration in finding the exact location of the dwelling they sought. But eventually, they spotted it.

What they saw could hardly be described as a house. 'Hovel' would have been a better word. Set against the mountain wall, it was built of stone with a flat, tiled roof. There was a single window, shuttered, and a door that looked rickety. A stub chimney projected from the rooftop, issuing wisps of greyish smoke. Moss and ivy smothered much of the exterior, and where it hadn't got ahold, cracks could be seen in the stonework. None of the angles seemed true. The impression was one of dilapidation, and Kye imagined that simply slamming the door might bring the whole structure down.

They approached warily, passing a small herb garden and a tiny plot of decorative flowering plants, many still to bud. The door, when they reached it, looked more substantial than at first sight, but that could have reflected their apprehension rather than its robustness. Kye hesitated.

"Well, go on then," Dyan said. "Or have we come all this way to be too scared to knock?"

"No, of course not. I was just wondering what kind of reception we'll get."

"Let's find out, shall we?" She gave the door a firm rap.

They waited. Nothing happened.

"Maybe she's not here," Kye suggested.

"It's getting late, she must be."

Kye tried, knocking louder.

Again, there was no response. They were at the point of thinking their journey had been wasted when they heard a bolt shoot. With a throaty creak, the door was opened, though nowhere near fully.

The person before them was small, but the interior was gloomy and they couldn't make out much more.

"What do you want?" The voice was identifiably feminine, but deep and gravelly.

"Are you Niola?" Kye asked.

"What if I am?"

"I'm sorry to disturb you. We're from Catterby and we seek your help."

"Not interested." The door began to close, their protests ignored. Then it stopped just short of fully shutting.

"Wait," said the woman, opening it again a fraction. "Stand a little back, young man, in the light, so I can see you properly."

Kye did as he was told.

"You had better come in," she said.

The interior resembled a cave, and apparently consisted of a single room. Such light as there was came from candles and a lone oil lamp. A log fire smouldered in the hearth, a small cauldron suspended above it. Bunches of drying plants hung from ceiling rafters, wobbly shelves held pots, bottles, and urns. Chests, clothes, and miscellaneous detritus were scattered everywhere. There was one chair, set near the fire. The place harboured a smell, or combination of smells, that were exotic, sweet, and heady, though not unpleasant.

As their eyes adjusted, they got their first clear view of the woman. She was old – old as time, it seemed to her young visitors. Her colourless hair was very thin and her face seemed to consist of nothing but wrinkles. She had no more than half a dozen teeth, and yellowing at that. Age had bent her back and gifted her with a shuffling gait.

"Thank you for seeing us," Kye said. "My name is—"

"I know who you are, Kye Beven. As I knew your father, for whom I offer my condolences. He was one of the better men in these parts. As was his father."

Kye was taken aback that she knew who he was, or that she somehow knew about the passing of his father, living as she did in such a remote spot. Somehow he didn't doubt that she could speak of his grandfather so knowingly, though Kye had never known him himself.

"Then you might know that our village faces a great peril," Dyan said.

"I am aware of that, Dyan Varike," Niola said, further confounding them.

"How do you know who we are?" Dyan asked.

"I know many things." She gave a wheezing laugh that ended in a brief coughing fit. When that was done she added, "Not least, I know of the dark forces brewing and the strands of evil threatening your village."

"Then will you help us?" Kye said.

"My inclination would be to say 'no'. The inhabitants of Catterby have never treated me very kindly and only visit, very rarely, when they want something, like a cure for themselves or their animals, or a love potion." She saw the disappointment in their faces.

"So you won't help us?"

"Had you been your village's Elder or one of your haughty council members, I would have no hesitation in leaving you to your fate. But your father, Kye Beven, showed me kindness and was never judgemental about the way I choose to live."

"So you *will* help?"

"If I can."

"I'm pleased to hear it. But how? A

spell, perhaps? Or—"

"No. There are limits to my powers. I can only help you to help yourselves."

"How does that work?"

"The answer lies within you."

"I don't understand."

"You will, when the time comes. Or else not, and all will be lost."

"I hope you'll forgive me for saying you talk in riddles," Dyan stated.

"Only to those who cannot hear. I have something for you. I've had it an age, waiting for something like this."

Niola went to a corner of the room and rummaged through a heap of her possessions, emerging with a long object wrapped in sacking and tied with twine.

She handed it to Kye.

"Thank you," he said. "What is it?"

"You can examine it at your leisure later," she told him firmly. "But remember this: to penetrate the heart of evil aim not at the power but at its source."

"But—"

"I am old and I'm tired. You will leave now."

She said it with such resolve that neither of them felt inclined to argue. Thanking her again, though they wondered why, they allowed themselves to be ushered out. The door closed behind them with a resounding thud. They walked away, puzzled and somewhat deflated.

"Look how dark it is now," Dyan

complained. "You'd think she might at least have offered us a place to sleep. So much for a wise old woman's hospitality."

"I'm not sure I'd have wanted to stay in that place. Anyway, it didn't look like she had the room."

"It's too late to start back now, and I don't relish the idea of travelling in the dark in these parts. Let's find somewhere to shelter for the night and start out early tomorrow."

"That's what I was thinking. And we'll take a look at this." He hefted the wrapped object.

As they searched for somewhere to spend the night, Dyan said, "Niola spoke about *the source of the power*. What does that mean? Isn't that Salex Nacandro?

And he's not likely to be riding into Catterby personally any time soon. How the hell are we supposed to get to him?"

"I don't know. I don't get it either. Maybe whatever's in this bundle will give us a clue."

Moving away from the foot of the mountain and into a slightly softer landscape, they located a spot in a grassy depression next to a stand of trees that offered some protection from the wind. They made themselves as comfortable as they could, grateful for having brought a little extra clothing.

"Right," Kye said, "let's take a look. Though from the feel of it I reckon I know what it is." He undid the twine and removed the sacking. Inside was another layer, this time of red silken cloth, which he unwound. "Yep, as I thought."

What was revealed was a bow. It was black and elegant, the curve of its limb most pleasing to the eye. They couldn't figure out what it was made of, except that it wasn't wood. Yet it was flexible and appeared strong although surprisingly light.

"It's beautiful," Dyan whispered.

"Yes. But when all's said and done, it's just a bow. Oh, and this." He retrieved an arrow, also black, from the silk wrapping.

"Only the one?"

"That's all there is."

Dyan pointed. "Notice those?"

On the stock and on the inside of

the limb were a series of symbols, very faded, that might once have been gold embellishments.

"Hmmm. Sort of ... glyphs, I suppose. Curious."

"You're disappointed, aren't you, Kye?"

"I'll admit that I was hoping for something more, though I don't know what. We have plenty of bows already."

"None as gracious as that."

"However it looks, a bow and a single arrow aren't going to make too much difference."

"Leave it be for now and rest. We should take turns sleeping, just to be on the safe side."

"Agreed. I'll take first watch."

He sat for a long time thinking about what Niola had said, and the significance, if any, of her gift.

※

They were awake and moving before dawn broke. The journey back was uneventful and they made good time. By late afternoon they were at Catterby.

The defences had been built up considerably in the short time they'd been away, and they had to negotiate two checkpoints to enter the village. As soon as he could, Kye made sure his mother was safe, while Dyan checked on several of her friends. They were reunited at one of the barricades, alongside Harper and a few other band members.

"That's a handsome bow," Harper commented.

Kye agreed that it was, but didn't try explaining how he got it. "I don't see Huew," he said.

"There's still no sign of him."

"Why am I reminded of the old saw about bullies being cowards?" Dyan mused.

There was a distant boom. "What was that?" she wondered.

"Whatever it was, it came from over there." Kye pointed.

The direction he indicated was where the checkpoints had been set up, and now there was a hint of fire there and smoke rising.

"Brace yourselves," Harper said. "This

is it."

There were further thunderous sounds and flames that grew taller and nearer. Once or twice a lightning-like flash of gold could be seen. Then a small group of horsemen came into sight.

"That's confidence for you," Harper remarked. "Unless they've got a contingent of warriors somewhere behind them, the Emissary's brought no more of his minions than last time."

"No," Kye corrected. "There are six this time, not five."

"And look who one of them is!" Dyan exclaimed.

They could see clearly now. The sixth horseman was Huew Rignorr.

"What the hell's he playing at?" Harper

wanted to know.

"I think we can guess," Kye said.

The horsemen drew up well short of the barricades.

Emissary Gudreen raised his arms and spoke. "So you choose to defy our lord! But be assured that your feeble resistance will make no difference, and the punishments meted out when we take control will be terrible indeed!"

Harper cupped his hands at his mouth and called out. "Huew! Huew Rignorr! What are you doing with these people?"

"I'm with them! And you should be too!"

"You treacherous bastard!"

"Call me what you will, but I'm not on the losing side! They offered me the

Eldership, and it's right that I should have it. My father was weak, like all the rest of you. Salex Nacandro and his followers bring strength."

"Heed him!" the Emissary said. "Follow his example and lay down your arms!"

Many voices answered, *"Never!"*

"Then if you won't yield I'll make you." His hand went up and the terrible beam flashed out, demolishing one of the barricades and consigning its defenders to flame.

The villagers fought back with arrows and spears. Two trebuchets had been constructed and they lobbed rocks at the invaders. But every missile dissipated at the invisible barrier protecting the men on horseback. At a gesture from the

Emissary, his minions began to move in.

"Have you noticed how those henchmen move, Kye?" Dyan said.

"What do you mean?"

They ducked as a golden beam streaked over their heads and destroyed a building to their rear.

"They move more or less in unison, stiffly, and in response to Gudreen's gestures. I reckon he's controlling them through magic in some way. They're linked."

"Could be." Kye released another arrow and watched it perish uselessly against the unseen barrier. "But I don't see how that helps us."

"Don't you? Remember what Niola said: *'To penetrate the heart of evil aim not at the power but at its source.'* Is this making sense?"

"I... I'm not sure."

"The *bow*, Kye, and the arrow that came with it. Have you used it yet?"

"No, it's here."

"Then nock it."

One of the trebuchets exploded, showering its makings on the villagers operating it. Timber and masonry rained down as buildings were sliced through by the lethal golden ray.

"What am I supposed to be targeting?" Kye asked.

"'*The heart of evil*,' remember? Try for that amulet the Emissary's wearing."

"That's a hell of a shot."

"Breathe," Harper contributed. "Take a breath and hold it. And remember what I said about your anchor point."

"I'll try." He took a look at his mark. The distance was about as far, perhaps further than any he'd ever shot. "I don't know that I can do this, and it looks like I only get one chance."

"Then make it count," Dyan insisted. "Remember what Niola said about finding the answer within yourself. Find that shot."

Kye drew the bow, aimed at the red-cored pendant at the Emissary's throat, and let loose. He fully expected the arrow to dissipate at any moment, like all the others.

But it didn't. It sailed straight to its

goal, unaffected by the magical protective cloak. An instant before it struck, the Emissary noticed its approach and knew the implications of its immunity to his magic. He screamed. The arrow smacked into the amulet and it shattered in a detonation of light that severely dazzled all those watching. A peal like thunder accompanied the brilliance, assaulting eardrums.

The Emissary toppled from his horse, quite dead, his chest raw and smoking. Simultaneously, his four henchmen dropped where they stood, their lives snapped off.

People were cheering and slapping backs.

"Well done, boy," Harper said. "Though perhaps I shouldn't call you that in future. You did well."

Dyan threw her arms around Kye. "That was a great shot! It's over, Kye, it's over!"

"Not quite." He looked out beyond the barricade and she followed his gaze.

Huew Rignorr sat on his horse, alone, surrounded by the corpses of his erstwhile allies. He looked perplexed, and as usual, angry.

Kye took an arrow from his quiver and nocked the wondrous bow. He drew, aimed, and sent it straight to Huew's heart, knocking him from the saddle. There were more cheers. Kye turned to Dyan and smiled.

"See?" she told him. "I said you could do it."

About the Author

Stan Nicholls is the author of more than thirty books and was shortlisted for the 2001 British Fantasy Award. His *Orcs: First Blood trilogy* is a worldwide bestseller, with over a million copies sold to date. Both Orcs trilogies made the *New York Times* bestseller list. Stan's books have been published in more than 20 countries.

He was the first manager of Forbidden Planet's original London store and helped establish and run the New York branch. He received the Le'Fantastique Lifetime Achievement Award for Contributions to Literature (2007).

Also by Stan Nicholls

Orcs: Omnibus Edition

Orcs Bad Blood: Second Omnibus Edition

Shake Me to Wake Me: The Best of
Stan Nicholls

Quicksilver Rising

… and more.

We would like to thank everyone who made this project possible,
via the Kickstarter and outside of it.

Specific thanks goes to:

Aaron Armitage

David Parker

Ross Warren

**More dyslexic friendly
titles coming soon...**

BOTH
PUBLISHING